Ellie Bear
and the
Fly-away Fly

ISBN 0-89272-335-1

Color Separations by Four Colour Imports
and by Graphic Color Service

Printed and bound at Arcata Graphics—Kingsport/Hawkins

5   4   3   2   1

DOWN EAST BOOKS / Camden, Maine

Library of Congress Cataloging-in-Publication Data

Rowinski, Kate, 1955–
    Ellie Bear and the fly-away fly / by Kate Rowinski ; illustrated by
Dawn Peterson.
        p.   cm.
    Summary: When Ellie Bear goes fishing with Uncle L.L., she
experiences adventure and a test of her own resourcefulness.
    ISBN 0-89272-335-1 ; $14.95
    [1. Fishing—Fiction. 2. Bears—Fiction. 3. Uncles Fiction.
4. Self-reliance—Fiction.] I. Peterson, Dawn, ill.   II. Title.
PZ7.R7969E1   1993
[E]—dc20
                                                        93-25260
                                                            CIP
                                                             AC

Ellie Bear
and the
Fly-away Fly

By Kate Rowinski

Illustrated by Dawn Peterson

Down East Books

*E*llie Bear climbed onto her uncle L.L. Bear's chair and peeked over his shoulder. "What are you doing?" she asked.

"I'm tying flies for our fishing trip!" said L.L. He held up a small brown speck. "See? We are going to use these to catch trout!"

"But those are just feathers!" Ellie squinted to get a better look at the little fly in her uncle's hand. "We can't catch any old fish with those!"

"Sure we can," he said. "We'll drop these flies onto the water using our fly rods. The fish will think they look like bugs and grab them."

L.L. hooked a fly onto the brim of her hat. "There you are, Ellie. That's my lucky fly. With that in your hat, you're a real fly-fisher. It will catch you some trout, all right."

Ellie smiled and put on her hat, patting it to make sure the fly was still there.

"Ready?" asked L.L., picking up his fly rod. "Off we go!"

The bears hiked through the woods until they reached the stream. Together, they watched it slide quicksilver over the rocks in its path.

"To be a fisher, Ellie, you must learn to think like a fish." L.L. looked out over the river. "Now, where do you think a fish might live?"

Ellie shook her head. "I don't know how fish think," she said.

L.L. pointed to a bird in the tree branch above them. "See that bird?" he said. "That's a kingfisher. It watches the river very closely. It has learned where the fish live and what their habits are. When a fish comes up to take an insect, the kingfisher will try to catch it!"

Suddenly the bird swooped down, dropping headfirst into the water. Ellie watched anxiously until it came to the surface again, empty-handed. The bird returned to the tree branch and shook the water from its feathers. Then it settled back onto the perch to continue its watch.

Ellie studied the river. She saw deep, still pockets of water and places where the water raced, bumpety-bumpety-bump, over the rocks. There were quiet, shadowy pools and bright, shallow runs with sandy bottoms. But she didn't see any fish. She sighed.

"Uncle L.L., why do you fish, anyway? Why don't you just buy fish at the market when you want to eat them?"

"Oh, I don't eat the fish I catch," replied L.L.

"You don't?"

"No, I fish for fun, and I put back the fish I catch, so when I leave the river, it's just the same as I found it."

"But fishing is *so much* trouble," said Ellie, glancing back at the bird. "If I catch a fish, I want to keep it."

"That's your right, Ellie. If you catch a fish, you may bring it home if you want."

Ellie nodded happily and ran scampering down the path, leaving her uncle to follow behind.

L.L. stopped by a pool where the river slipped quietly through the shadows of an old oak tree. "See?" he whispered. "This is a good place to live if you're a trout. There are bugs dropping down from the trees, and nice deep water to keep you cool and safe. If we wait a minute, we just might see one."

The bears were very quiet. After a few moments, they heard a quiet *shloop* as a small brook trout sipped an insect off the top of the water. The little fish barely made a sound, but it left behind a small round ripple that grew and grew before disappearing completely.

"Ahhhh!" L.L. chuckled. "Someone does live here. He's pretty small though. Why don't we get out our fishing gear? I want to find some big fish."

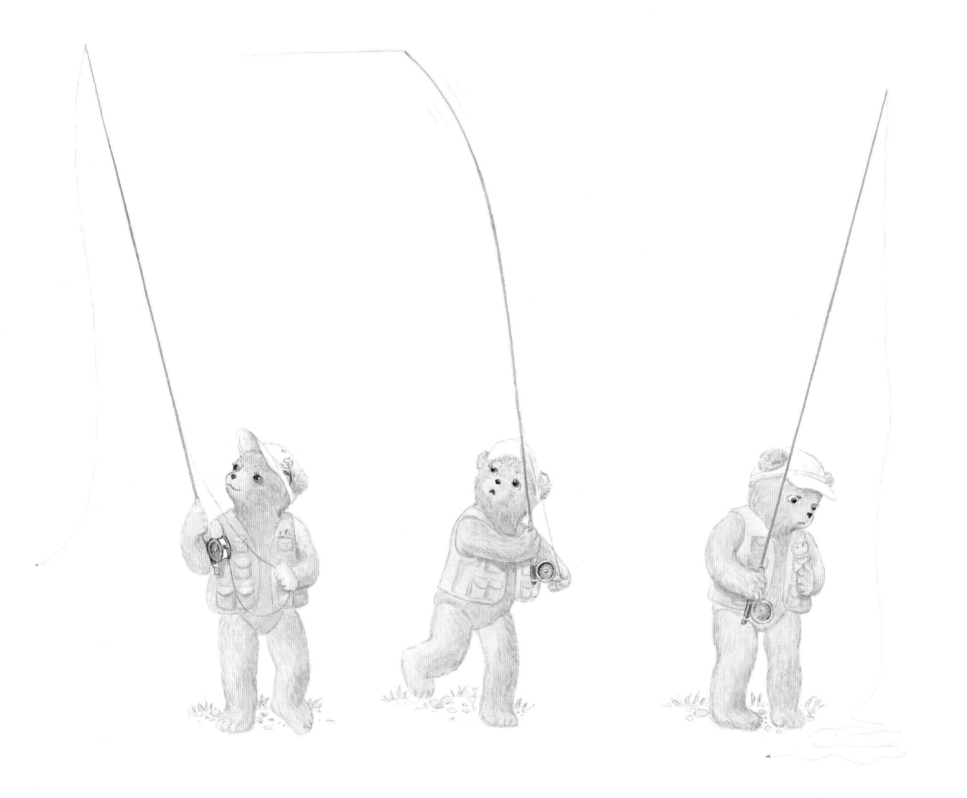

L.L. helped Ellie put on her fishing vest and tied a bright fly to the end of her line. Then he showed her how to make the fly drop lightly onto the surface of the water.

Ellie tried to do what her uncle showed her, but it wasn't easy. First her fly got tangled in the trees behind her, then the line fell into a jumble at her feet.

"I'll never get it right!"

"Take it slowly," said L.L. "I had the same trouble when I was your age." He put his paw over hers and guided the rod smoothly over the water. The fly landed without a sound.

"Good! Now watch very carefully. When you see a fish, be ready!"

Ellie watched her fly closely, but didn't see any fish come to look. She picked up the line and cast again and again, holding her breath as she waited. But nothing happened.

Ellie waded back to shore and threw down her fly rod. "I can't think like a fish!" she yelled. "I don't want to catch any old fish anyway!" She kicked at a rock, sending a spray of sand and pebbles into the river. "There probably aren't any fish in this river."

L.L. laughed. "Take that fly from your hat, Ellie. That one is sure to fool a fish. It looks just like the bugs they are eating." He took the fly and tied it to her line. Then he handed Ellie the rod and picked up his gear. "I'll go downstream to fish," he said. "You take this spot. It looks like trout water to me."

"Okay," said Ellie reluctantly, watching her uncle disappear around the bend. She waded into the river and cast her line into the stream. "But I don't know why *anybody* would bite on a mouthful of feathers!"

SPLASH! Something dropped like a torpedo from the sky. The water exploded around Ellie's fly. "Oh Gosh! I've got one!" she yelled. "I've got a—"

SPLASH! The kingfisher broke the surface of the water and flew straight into the air, carrying Ellie's fly away.

"—a bird?" Ellie watched in amazement as the bird flew back to the tree, trailing her fly line behind.

She tugged on the line, causing a loud *SQUAWK* and a frantic flapping of wings high in the tree. The fly was tangled in the bird's feathers!

Ellie put her rod and reel down on the riverbank and made her way toward the tree. She saw the bird at the very end of a branch, hopping up and down angrily. She climbed toward it.

Ellie could see her fly hooked in the bird's wing. The line was tangled in the branches, making it impossible for it to fly away.

"What a clever bird!" Ellie said in a soothing voice. "You missed the fish, but you caught my fly!" She reached her hand slowly toward the bird and unhooked the fly. "Too bad about the hook, though. I'm sorry you got poked!"

She held up the hook for the kingfisher to see. The bird ruffled its feathers indignantly and flew away in search of less dangerous fish.

Ellie pulled the line from the nearby branch, remembering too late that it was still attached to the rod and reel. The rod slipped into the river and began to float downstream.

"Oh, no!" cried Ellie, scrambling to gather up the line. "Oh, help!"

She snatched at the rod and missed, almost losing her balance. All she could do now was cling to the tree branch, watching miserably as the rod drifted away, breaking the line she still held in her hand.

Tears stung Ellie's eyes. She tried to scoot back along the branch, but she was afraid to loosen her grip. She was stuck.

A quiet *shloop, shloop* caught Ellie's attention. She opened her eyes and wiped away her tears. The little trout in the pool below was eating lunch.

From her bird's-eye view, Ellie saw how the fish waited for bugs to land on the water. She saw it sneak up quietly and snatch them with its strong jaws. She watched it swim back and forth in rhythm with the ripples of water that played over its back.

Ellie remembered her own fly, still tied to the end of her line. She pulled it out and dangled it over the stream. When the little fish came to look at it, she quickly pulled it away.

Ellie laughed. She tried different ways of moving the fly around, skittering it along the surface like a waterbug and splashing it loudly like a grasshopper. The fish tried again and again to grab the fly. Before long, Ellie was so busy with her game that she forgot all about being stranded in the tree. She loosened her grip on the branch a little, stretching to place the fly right over the fish's nose.

SLAP! The fish grabbed Ellie's fly and dived deep under the water with it, pulling her right off the branch. She tumbled into the river with a *SPLASH!* The fish leaped and twisted and jumped as Ellie struggled to hold on to the line.

Meanwhile, Ellie's rod and reel had bumped slowly downstream to the next pool, where L.L. was fishing. He plucked it out of the water and came running to see what had happened.

"Ellie!" he called. "Are you all right? Why are you in the water?"

Ellie came up to the surface, sputtering and laughing. "Yes, I'm fine. I was just thinking like a fish! And look, I caught a trout!"

L.L. helped her to her feet, then grabbed his fishing net. "Slip him into the net, Ellie," he said. "He's a brave little fish, but he's getting tired."

The trout lay still in the net, its colors shining like jewels against the dark water. "Why, that's the prettiest trout I've ever seen!" he said.

"He's beautiful," whispered Ellie.

"Do you want to take him home?"

"No," she told her uncle. "I want to let him go."

L.L. leaned down and slipped the hook from the fish's mouth. "Hold him for a moment."

Ellie held the little brook trout between her hands, rocking it back and forth in the water until it started to move.

"He's ready now," said her uncle.

Ellie let go. The fish paused for a moment, then with a flip of its tail, it was gone. Ellie watched the place in the water where the trout had disappeared.

"What made you decide to let him go?" L.L. asked.

"I guess I just want him to be here next time I come," she said, smiling.

The two bears took one last look at the river before turning for home. They saw the little trout come up and sip a newly hatched insect off the surface. Then it disappeared again, into the cool water of the deep pool under shady tree branches, where mayflies danced and ripples of water played over its back.